A Pumpkin Story

To my husband, Akio Shinju

A Pumpkin Story

Text copyright © 1998 Mariko Shinju.
Illustrations © 1998 by Mariko Shinju.
Typography by Alicia Mikles.
All rights reserved including the right of reproduction
in whole or in part in any from. Printed in Hong Kong.
For information address: Greene Bark Press
PO Box 1108 Bridgeport, CT 06601-1108

Publisher's Catalog-in-Publication
(Provided by Quality Books Inc.,)

Shinju, Mariko
    A Pumpkin Story / written and illustrated by Mariko
Shinju -- 1st ed.
    p. cm.
    SUMMARY: A man in a poor village finds and plants
some pumpkin seeds. Soon there are so many enormous pumpkins in the village that the people can eat their fill and even
construct homes from the pumpkins.
    Preassigned LCCN: 98-71912
    ISBN: 1-880851-36-9

    1. Pumpkin--Juvenile fiction. 2. Pumpkin--Seeds--
Juvenile fiction. Title.

PZ7.S556Pu 1998   [E]
                                   QB198.793

A Pumpkin Story

written and illustrated by

MARIKO SHINJU

GREENE BARK PRESS

ONCE UPON A TIME, there was a very poor man who lived in a very poor village. Everyday he went into the mountains to find food to eat.

One day, he was walking along a mountain path. Suddenly he saw some seeds on the ground. "Oh, my!," he said, "Those look like pumpkin seeds." He picked up a handful, took them home, and sowed them in the fields around his small house.

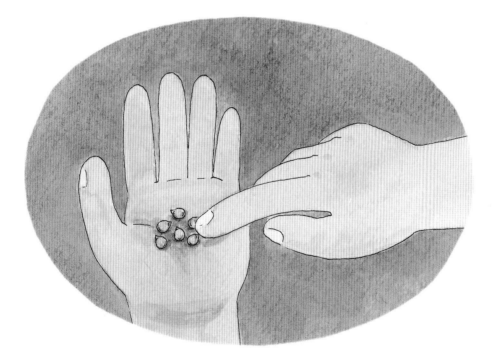

He watered the seeds everyday, and the seeds soon pushed up new shoots and young leaves. They grew quickly, and small pumpkins soon appeared.

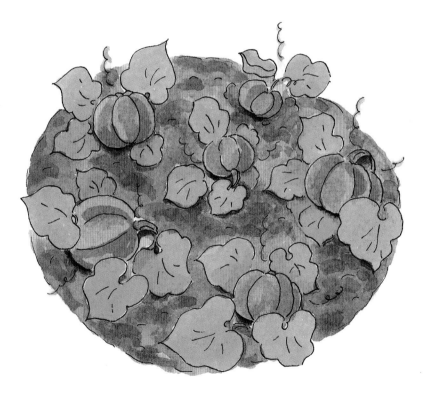

Gratefully, he collected the pumpkins, scooped out
the seeds, and made hot pumpkin soup for dinner. The next
day, he sowed more of the seeds into the fields. He watered
them everyday. The pumpkins grew quickly.

Everyday he ate hot pumpkin soup. One day, he made a special candle holder out of one perfect little pumpkin. In it, he placed his only candle, to add warm light to his house at night. In the morning, he went again to sow seeds in his fields.

Every time he planted new seeds the
pumpkins grew bigger and bigger. More and
more pumpkins grew on each vine. His pumpkins
were soon bigger than his head!

He began to make other nice things. He scooped the pumpkins out and dried them to make pots, soup bowls and cups.

By and by, his pumpkins grew bigger and bigger. He made a pumpkin bed and a pumpkin bath tub. Finally, he made a pumpkin house! It was full of beautiful things. Everything was made of pumpkins . . .

When he didn't need anything else for himself, he gave his pumpkin seeds to other people in his village. They were also poor and hungry, so they were delighted with their new pumpkin dinners, pots, and pumpkin houses.

Everyone in the village soon lived in pumpkin houses.
Thankfully, pumpkins kept growing bigger and bigger.
Everyone's stomach was full.

Then the villagers and the pumpkin man decided to make a pumpkin hotel of their best pumpkins. They worked hard to scoop out the insides of huge pumpkins and made elegant pumpkin furniture of others. Everyone looked forward to the opening day. . . .

Soon the big day came, and people from near and far came to stay at the pumpkin hotel. In no time at all, the village became famous as the pumpkin village.

While moms and dads enjoyed the concert of the pumpkin band, their children swam and played in the pumpkin pool.

At the end of each day, sight-seers ate special pumpkin puddings, delicious pumpkin pies, crusty pumpkin bread, and of course, the famous pumpkin soup!

Before going to sleep in pumpkin beds, everyone enjoyed taking pumpkin baths.

The fame of the pumpkin hotel in the pumpkin village grew and grew. At night the pumpkin man looked out over the village and smiled. No one was poor or hungry anymore. Everyone had a comfortable house and good food to eat. They now could all live happily and peacefully forever.